Henry Duff Traill

Recaptured Rhymes

being a batch of political and other fugitives arrested and brought to book

Henry Duff Traill

Recaptured Rhymes
being a batch of political and other fugitives arrested and brought to book

ISBN/EAN: 9783337271510

Printed in Europe, USA, Canada, Australia, Japan

Cover: Foto ©Andreas Hilbeck / pixelio.de

More available books at **www.hansebooks.com**

RECAPTURED RHYMES:

BEING

A BATCH OF POLITICAL AND OTHER FUGITIVES

ARRESTED AND BROUGHT TO BOOK

BY

H. D. TRAILL

WILLIAM BLACKWOOD AND SONS
EDINBURGH AND LONDON
MDCCCLXXXII

N O T E.

OF the pieces of verse collected into this volume, the greater number are reprinted from the 'St James's Gazette.' Of the remainder, four were contributed to the 'Pall Mall Gazette' before the change which took place in its proprietary and direction on the 3d of May 1880; two appeared in the 'World;' six in 'Time;' and one, "The Ant's Nest," in the 'Fortnightly Review.'

The Author takes this oppo: proprietors of these periodicals for the permission to republish.

CONTENTS.

POLITICAL VERSE.

OCCASIONAL RHYMES.

MIMICRIES.

POST LUSUS, SERIA.

POLITICAL VERSE

LAPUTA OUTDONE.

Oh, Philosopher crazed from the Island of Crazes,
    Explored and depicted by Jonathan Swift,
Let us hear what your judgments on us and our ways
        is—
    Permit us your mental impressions to sift.

For *we* have our follies of wisdom fantastic,
    Some high-philosophic, political some,
And would fain ascertain, in no spirit sarcastic,
    If you, my dear pundit, can match them at home.

When a man in Laputa falls sick unto danger,
    Then is it the rule in that singular place
To throw up the window and ask the first stranger
    To kindly come in and prescribe on the case?

When in legal perplexities, slighter or deeper,
   For counsel in law a Laputan applies,
Does he seek the next crossing and beg of its sweeper,
   When business is done, to step round and advise?

Are your pilots' certificates commonly given
   To men who have not even looked on the seas?
Are your coachmen selected for not having driven?
   Say, have you Laputans got customs like these?

You haven't? Then off with your bee-bearing bonnet,
   Illustrious guest from Luggnaggian shores!
And down on your knee and do homage upon it
   Profound to a State that is madder than yours!

For though we select not attorney, physician,
   Or pilot who steers us, or coachman who drives,
From the ignorant crowd, who would gain erudition
   At risk of our fortunes, our limbs, or our lives;

Yet this Ignorance dense that we do not let lead us
  In private concerns, lest disaster befall,
This, that may not make wills for us, dose us, or bleed
    us
  May *rule* us—the business that's hardest of all!

We say to It " Courage !   Nay, go not so shyly !
  In time you will master the work you are at ;
Your country presents you her own *corpus vile,*
  See, here is the commonweal, practise on that !

" Away with the notion (we echo in chorus)
  Of power withheld until knowledge be gained,"
(Too long, cry the carts, have the horses before us
  Unjust and unworthy precedence obtained !)

" The use of the scalpel in surgical functions
  Will give you the skill of a surgeon professed,
And by much engine-driving at intricate junctions
  One learns to drive engines along with the best."

For is it not thus our political preachers
    Discourse to us daily, in bidding us note
That "the franchise itself is the truest of teachers,"
    That "voting instructs in the use of the vote"?

So, off with it!   Off with your bee-bearing bonnet,
    Illustrious guest from Luggnaggian shores!
And down on your knee, and do homage upon it
    Profound to a State that is madder than yours!

THE BARON DE WIGG.

ALL ye who sit waiting in moody array,
Oppositionists eager to welcome a day
　　With the fate of the Ministry big,
Chastise your passion for power and place
By recalling the sad but instructive case
　　Of the fine old Baron de Wigg.

Old Baron de Wigg from his earliest years
Had moved in the highest official spheres,
　　Until he had learnt to dream
That "placemen" and "Wiggs" were convertible terms,
And belonged to a system of which the germs
　　Formed part of the cosmic scheme.

He considered the ends of creation gained
On the whole, while De Wiggs high office retained,

  Fulfilment complete being won
When the head of the house was the realm's chief guide,
And each of the other De Wiggs supplied

  With a post for a younger son.

Now imagine the Baron de Wigg's disgust
At finding the family suddenly thrust

  From their natural place in the State
By men who from '32 down to that hour
Had never enjoyed a spell of power

  Of more than the briefest date.

But as year after year kept slipping away,
To disgust there began a profound dismay

  In the Baron's breast to succeed ;
For, if longer excluded from place, he saw
That the uniform order of physical law

  Could hardly be guaranteed.

This gloomy conviction inclined him to lend
Too willing an ear to a dubious friend
    (Mr Latterday Radd was his name),
Who offered the Baron his counsel and aid
To regain what was worthy the prize to be made
    Of a slightly unscrupulous game.

But Latterday Radd two acquaintances had,
Who rejoiced in the names of Crotchett and Fadd—
    A quite unpresentable pair;
And the Baron, who could not afford to contemn
An alliance with Radd, thought mixing with *them*
    To be—well, quite another affair.

So when in pure zeal for De Wigg and his ends,
Radd promised to drop his unsavoury friends
    (To " sink " was the word he employed),
The Baron was touched by the simple young man
Who such loyalty showed to himself and his clan,
    And accepted his aid overjoyed.

And all the De Wiggs were effusive in praise
Of the truly high-minded magnanimous ways
    Of good Mr Latterday Radd,
And the disinterested effacement of self
With which their consent to be laid on the shelf
    Had credited Crotchett and Fadd.

By the help of the friend enlisted so
(The while his associates shy " lay low,"
    According to pledge and resolve)
The De Wiggs regained their official berth,
And the planets returned to their paths, and the earth
    Began once more to revolve.

But his conquest of place was no sooner achieved
Than the Baron next day to his horror perceived—
    Arm-linked with Latterday Radd—
That obtrusive old Crotchett pervading the place,
And behind them the pert and self-satisfied face
    Of the still more odious Fadd.

De Wigg would have cut them and hurried away,
But Radd was before him, and hastened to say
    In a coldly imperious tone:
" Permit me, dear Baron—(don't try to look big):
Mr Fadd, Mr Crotchett—the Baron de Wigg,
    The friends of your friend are your own."

On the Baron expressing in manner constrained
Surprise at their presence, his friend explained
    That his pledge had been misunderstood;
For a time—and a purpose—he said, 'twas true,
He had promised to " sink " the obnoxious two,
    But never to sink them for good.

De Wigg having risen they too must rise,
And he, as a friend, would the Baron advise
    To be civil to Crotchett and Fadd;
So the Baron shook hands with a ghastly smile,
For he fully admitted the need, for a while,
    Of, at least, being civil to Radd.

Thus *lancés* and thus influentially backed,
The pair to this wretched old party are tacked,
    And declare, on advancement intent,
That he *must* introduce them without more ado
In both the great Houses he's access unto ;
    And the Baron will have to consent.

All ye, then, who sit in impatient array,
Oppositionists eager to welcome a day
    With the fate of the Ministry big,
Chastise your passion for power and place
By recalling the sad but instructive case
    Of the fine old Baron de Wigg.

BALLAD OF BALOONATICS CRANIOCRACS.

OF all the accomplished Professors who ever
From learning contrived common-sense to dissever—
Of all who delight, on a question of tongue,
To foment agitation the peoples among—
None goes with such thoroughness into the thing
As the erudite Slav whose proceedings I sing ;
And whose name—if your jaws I may venture to tax—
Is Professor Baloonatics Craniocracs.

International law has his sovereign contempt ;
From restraints of political prudence exempt,
He holds that when races for union clamour,
The question's but one of comparative grammar.

No " national movement," whatever its fruits,
That starts from a real relation of roots,
The strenuous aid and encouragement lacks
Of the famous philologist, Craniocracs.

To many a cause of the " national " sort
The Professor has lent his enlightened support;
But of all his distinctions, his pride was to be a
High priest of the Pan-Macaronic Idea,
And first to have raised the Spaghettian claim
To inherit the true Macaronian name :
A position sustained against many attacks
By Professor Baloonatics Craniocracs.

The Spaghetts had been living in decent content, a
Race subject for centuries past to Polenta,
With liberties local and customs respected,
And lenient taxes with justice collected,

And ample permission their children to teach
That poetic and grandly cacophonous speech
Which first to their true nationality's tracks
Had directed Baloonatics Craniocracs.

But they, when he set their ethnology right,
With the free Macaronians burned to unite :
And the worthy Professor went round through their
    cities
Establishing Pan-Macaronic Committees,
Until they rebelled in a war to the knife,
And after two years of the bloodiest strife,
Forced haughty Polenta her grasp to relax,
To the joy of their champion Craniocracs.

From this struggle the rise of the Union dates
Of the Pan-Macaronic Confederate States,
Which, besides the Spaghetts, of a kindred as true
Raviolians counts and Lasagnians too.

But above them the Pateditalians claim
A supremacy, due to generical name ;
And their claim the Professor unswervingly backs,
For philologist always is Craniocracs.

Are the freed populations content with their lot ?
Well, candour compels me to say they are not.
Already the Union is deeply in debt
And taxed to the skin is the wretched Spaghett.
And the Pateditalians forbid him to teach
His poetic and grandly cacophonous speech,
On the ground that of modern corruption it smacks—
As is even admitted by Craniocracs.

But the worst of it is (if the murder must out),
The Professor's researches have led him to doubt
If his first ethnologic conclusions were sound,
Since he, as it seems, a new " factor " has found,

The " Vermicellenic," so named from a race
Whose affinities throw a new light on the case ;
Transforming, indeed, into whites all its blacks
To the mind of Baloonatics Craniocracs.

Through the Vermicellenes the Spaghett and his
   · brother,
Are clearly of kin to Polenta and other
Great nations ; and though they could only unite
By involving the world in a general fight,
The Professor, intrepid of logic as ever,
Will work day and night at that noble endeavour.
All hobbies are wild, but the wildest of hacks
Is bestrid by Baloonatics Craniocracs.

AN ENFANT TERRIBLE.

I.

THE baby was born on a lowering morn
　In Seventeen Eighty-and-Nine,
And poets and sages enacted the Mages
　Who hailed the event divine.

Their " star in the west " had, it must be confessed,
　A slightly sulphureous gleam ;
But it faithfully led to the tumble-down shed,
　At the sign of " The Old Régime."

The adorers brought of the gold of Thought,
　And the myrrh and frankincense of Song ;
And they worshipped the birth that redeemed the earth
　From the Old Dispensation of wrong.

With each other they vied for the pleasure and pride
    Of preparing the Prince's crown,
And every one smiled on the infant mild
    Till he kicked—and the house fell down.

II.

Then the poets and sages who acted as Mages
    Went home to consider the scene,
And with serious looks sat them down to their books
    To resolve what this portent should mean.

And when they had found upon reasoning sound
    What the strange new thing must be,
They compared their notes, and collected the votes,
    And it seemed that they couldn't agree.

Some courageously said a mistake had been made,
    That the good they had worshipped was evil,
Their Saviour supposed, by his conduct disclosed
    For an obvious limb of the Devil.

But others demurred to this view, and preferred
　　A conclusion less humbling to pride,
And admitting the child to be wayward and wild,
　　His Satanic extraction denied.

'Twas (they said) premature to affect to be sure
　　How a babe later on will behave,
And for all that the boy had begun to destroy,
　　It might well be his mission to save.

III.

But to common surprise, while disputed the wise,
　　Was the infant inspired or mad,
To boyhood 'twas reared, and it shortly appeared
　　That the world was too small for the lad.

He had got him a blade at Ajaccio made,
　　And had picked up a song at Marseilles,
And had rigged up a flag from a three-coloured rag
　　He had fixed to its staff—with nails.

A bonnet of red he had cocked on his head,

   Steel-bright were his eyes, and wild ;

Unkempt was his hair, and his legs were bare—

   A truly unusual child !

IV.

So sallied he forth, East, South, and North,

   To the barren lands and the fair ;

To the South in its glows, to the North in its snows,

   To the East in its desert-glare.

To the Elbe, to the Rhine, through the plumed Apen-

     nine,

   Over Italy's plains he hastes;

Then Eastward far—till his conquering star

   Grew dim on the Syrian wastes:

To the shores of the Nile ; to the Knights' old isle ;

   Then again by the pierced Pyrenees,

South, south, ever south, to the Mid-sea's mouth,

   At the Pillars of Hercules.

East, North, and South, as a flood to its mouth
    Bears trees of the forest uptorn,
On the towering crest of the wave in his breast
    Was the terrible urchin borne.

With the spilth of his hands he slaked the sands
    Athirst of Egyptian suns ;
He scarred the scalp of the frozen Alp
    With the wheels of his clambering guns. '

Sank hearts of kings when rustled the wings
    Of his eagles about their ears ;
At his cannon-knell old empires fell,
    And thrones of a thousand years.

All wisdom of time, all strength of prime,
    At the foot of this stripling crude,
With his head in a blaze of its single craze,
    Lay stupefied, spent, subdued !

V.

And the doctors ?   Well, if the truth be to tell,
   Even some in opinion stout,
Who had clung to the creed that the child was indeed
   A Messiah, began to doubt.

But the sturdiest ones still stuck to their guns,
   And maintained his legation divine ;
" Not peace, but a sword," was the scriptural word,
   From which he had taken his line.

Then the kings he o'erthrew had had only their due,
   And might even a punishment worse
Have deservedly got for a certain vile plot,
   To strangle the baby at nurse.

VI.

Thus the doctors cried ; but the world outside,
   That life, not books, understands—
The Great Commonplace—had already the case
   Withdrawn from the doctors' hands.

To the men of the field and the mart was revealed,
  Through a mist of conceptions vague,
One truth, clear as light, that, cost what it might,
  They must promptly abate this plague.

So the nations clubbed, that the boy might be drubbed;
  While he, with unwavering mind,
Stood, a new Athanase—would the whole world face
  For a creed—of a different kind.

He fought hard and hot, and with varying lot,
  And with hopes now high, now low,
Till a certain forenoon, in the month of June,
  When he closed with his strongest foe.

They closed, and the shock made Europe to rock,
  And the pulse of her heart to stay,
While the wrestlers gasped, in their death-grip clasped,
  For all one breathless day.

But his glass was run ; sank, sank with the sun
    The line of its lessening sand,
And as night came down he was prostrate thrown,
    And the great sword torn from his hand.

This, safe under lock, on a sea-girt rock
    They hid ; and it six years lay
Condemned to rust in the island dust,
    Till it rusted its heart away.

While as for the boy who had wrought such annoy
    To the world in his youthful fling,
Of his ways to repent, straight home he was sent
    In charge of a Christian King.

They tore down his rag of a tricolor flag,
    And they gave him a banner instead,
Of a beautiful white, with lilies bedight,
    And gold for the blue and the red.

They put him to school of the good priests' rule,
    To atone by penance and praise
And prostration of soul for his Carmagnole,
    And mass for his Marseillaise.

VII.

In this excellent way (so the doctors say)
    Was the scapegrace led to reform ;
And a grave middle age, respected and sage,
    Has succeeded his youth of storm.

And (excepting, perhaps, one unlucky relapse
    From his later regenerate state,
Into juvenile ways on the great Three Days,
    And another in 'forty-eight,

And a third—worst far—at the end of the War)
    He has yearly become more staid ;
More and more like that other, his English brother,
    Who's fat, and has taken to trade.

And though, here and there, some devil-may-care
 Of a Russ or a *Bursch* by the Spree
May claim him as kin, they will shortly begin
 Oats sown, to reform, just as he.

VIII.

Thus the doctors declare with their confident air ;
 But many there be who avow
That, for all they have seen of thy altered mien,
 O Democracy, dread art thou !

If their fancy essay thy form to portray,
 In the vision that faces them then,
No shape they behold of the stature and mould
 Of a man among mortal men.

But rather in thought is thy emblem wrought
 Mysterious, formless, vast ;
A giant of stone on a giant throne,
 Like the gods of the long-buried past.

Yet about thy feet light chatterers meet,
   Politician and pamphleteer,
And they learnedly prose on the form of thy toes
   Or the toe which may chance to be near.

Not caring to raise their complacent gaze
   So high that a glance may fall
On the hands laid at ease o'er the monstrous knees—
   Those hands which could cover us all!

Not caring to trace on the stone-hewn face,
   With its distance-questioning eyes,
That inscrutable smile of the Head by the Nile
   That is dumb till the sun shall rise.

When its first rays smite, what chord of affright
   Will it sound for the world's new song?
What ground-tone of fear?—Who lives, he shall hear:
   May *he* not have lived too long!

THE REGION OF DREAM.

In a legend of old 'tis recorded for us
   That the air and the sea and the land
To the children of man were distributed thus
   By Zeus his apportioning hand:

He appointed the land for the Workers to share,
   And the sea for the Poet to roam,
But assigned in his wisdom the vacuous air
   For the Higher Philosopher's home.

" Go wander," said Zeus to this last (we were taught),
   " Where alone there is room for your schemes,
In a region as wide as the reach of your thought,
   And as lofty—and void—as your dreams.

" Here is food for your mind, for your body a feast
  Of the which never dearth can befall,
Ay, a plenty of nourishing wind from the East
  To fill you your belly withal.

" From the clouds you may gather your theory-stuff,
  Definitions from tracks of the birds,
Here are mists in abundance and more than enough
  For becomingly clothing your words.

" Here perform at your leisure the feats that you love
  Unrestrained by conditions of place,
And leap from the plane where your premisses move
  To conclusions in Infinite Space.

" I will give you, to deck your magnificent views,
  The run of the rainbow-span,
And allow you the pick of the sunset hues
  To adorn your ' Future-of-Man,' "

Thus Zeus, in the legend, ordained it, and hence
    Mankind have been wont to declare
Of all Theory freed from the trammels of sense,
    That its natural home is the air.

But *now* would you know the Chimera's abode,
    And the kingdom of Folly Supreme ?
Would you seek, in these days, to discover the road
    To the genuine region of dream ?

It is not in the vacuous air, it is not
    In the wandering clouds, wind-blown.
The region of dream is the three-acre plot
    Where an Irishman's " praties " are sown.

It is here where the eye philosophic detects
    The suspension of natural laws ;
Where causes omit to engender effects
    And effects can dispense with a cause.

It is here where the marvels of magical spell
   Medieval find credit once more,
And "peasant-proprietor" conjures as well
   As an "Abracadabra" of yore.

It is here, it is here, on the Irishman's farm
   Where alchemic economists hold
That to utter the "peasant-proprietor" charm
   Transmutes the base metals to gold,

That by force of this sorcery Waste becomes Thrift
   And energy springs out of Sloth,
That the burden of Need reappears as a gift
   And exhaustion of soil as a growth.

Ah! bodiless, limitless regions of space!
   What dream have you brought to the birth
So fantastic as this whose nativity-place
   Is the solid, dull, definite earth?

OCCASIONAL RHYMES

HONI SOIT QUI MAL Y PENSE.

(Brighton. 1881.)

SCENE.—*A Railway Platform. Policemen assembled. To them an Inspector : they exchange greetings. He sings, accompanying himself softly on the Rattle.*

INSPECTOR.

Heed not, comrades, though they taunt us
    With the Frenchman's subtler art ;
'Tis a prouder boast to vaunt us
    In the wisdom of the heart.

Be it ours—we much prefer it—
    To survey men's works and ways
In a nobler, kindlier spirit,
    With a franker, freer gaze.

Higher heights of moral stature
Presuppose a wider glance ;
Let us trust in human nature,
  " Honi soit qui mal y pense."

Doubt, we know, is from the devil,
  Let us thrust its lures aside ;
Constables who think no evil
  Ever have been England's pride.

ALL *(enthusiastically)*.

Ay ! away with base suspicion,
  And with thoughts that wrong mankind !
Ill it were in our position
  To indulge a cynic mind.

(A train enters the station.   They approach it.)

INSPECTOR.

See from yonder railway carriage
  Who is this emerging, pray,

In a plight 'twould scarce disparage
    To describe as disarray ?

Why ! his face and hands are gory,
    And exhausted he appears !
Stranger, pour your moving story
    In our sympathetic ears.

(He pours it.)

ALL.

Ah, most startling !   Ah, most thrilling !
    Of romance 'tis strangely full !
Aged merchant—missing villain—
    Countryman—and cock-and-bull !

INSPECTOR (*after a pause*).

Yet I fain would ask you, stranger,
    How—but, no, this will not do ;
Mutual trust it might endanger—
    Who am I to question *you ?*

ALL (*approvingly*).

Who, indeed ?   Avaunt, suspicion !
   Down, ye thoughts that wrong mankind !
Ill befits it our position
   To indulge a cynic mind.

      (*Another pause, during which they eye*
         the stranger closely.)

INSPECTOR (*after a struggle with himself*).

Pardon, Sir, the strong desire I
   Vainly labour to restrain ;
But th' old Adam of inquiry
   Rises in my breast again.

Tell me (thus a weakness lingers !)
   How and when you tore your coat ;
And are those not marks of fingers
   That I see upon your throat ?

Where's your collar? where your necktie?
   Where—but why the question press?
If your *mens* be *conscia recti*
   What's a collar more or less?

ALL.

What, indeed?   Away, suspicion!
   Get thee, Satan's child, behind!
Let us each in his position
   Shun that curse—a cynic mind.

(Yet another pause. They still continue
eyeing the stranger.)

INSPECTOR (*diffidently*).

I despise the art of angling
   For disclosures—mean pursuit!·
But . . . . I notice something dangling
   (Not a bootlace) from your boot.

Ha! a watch-chain! I declare, it
  Seems a funny place to—eh?
What! "The way you always wear it?"
  Say no more! forgive me, pray!

True-born Britons never heed 'em,
  Casual trifles such as these;
Heirs to centuries of freedom
  Wear their watch-chains how they please.

ALL (*proudly*).

True! Away then, vile suspicion!
  Spurn we thoughts that wrong mankind!
Base it were in our position
  To indulge a cynic mind.

INSPECTOR.

Now farewell! the word may grieve us
  Yet at last we must dismiss
Dearest friends; but ere you leave us
  Gentle stranger, tell me this:

Since we may your kind assistance
  Need to trace this dreadful crime—
Are you going any distance?
  Or for any length of time?

" Just a week of foreign travel ? "
  Thanks ! Then we may count on you
After that to help unravel
  This dark mystery ! Adieu !

> (*Stranger embraces the police, beginning
> with the Inspector ; then enters a Con-
> tinental train. They watch it moving
> from the station until it is lost to view.*)

INSPECTOR and CHORUS.

Speed thee, speed thee, o'er the billow !

  I
  We $\Big\}$ will *not* believe thee vile.

Smooth, O smooth is strewn the pillow
  Under heads that know no guile.

Doubt, $\left.{\begin{matrix} \text{I} \\ \text{We} \end{matrix}}\right\}$ feel, is from the devil;

$\left.{\begin{matrix} \text{I will} \\ \text{Let us} \end{matrix}}\right\}$ thrust its lures aside.

Constables that think no evil

Ever have been England's pride.

FROM AN IRISH LETTER-BAG.

(1880.)

DEAR FRANK,

    I have read with profound admiration
      The eloquent speeches you lately have made,
    And applaud in especial that noble oration
      Directed at landlords who wish to be paid.

    You denounce with the force of invincible reason
      Those merciless men who their tenantry press,
    And who thus in the present deplorable season
      Attempt to make capital out of distress.

    Of the part that I took at the recent election
      To aid your return I have cause to be proud;
    So believe me, dear Frank, with the truest affection,
      Yours ever admiringly,

                DICKY O'DOWD.

DEAR DICK,

    For the friendly and cousinly spirit

        Displayed in your letter its writer I thank ;

    Of landlords like you the approval to merit

        Is more than enough for yours heartily,

                                    FRANK.

DEAR FRANK,

    I have no hesitation in tasking

        The kindness of one so large-hearted as you,

    And I therefore address you with confidence, asking

        Your leave for delaying a payment that's due.

    As from now till a year from the coming December

        The rent of my farms I must wholly abate,

    You will hardly expect me till then to remember

        Your charge on the Ballymahoony estate.

Hard pressed as I am, it would greatly relieve me,

 This eighteen months' grace if I might be allowed ;

So, assuming your friendly forbearance, believe me,

 Your cousin affectionate,

DICKY O'DOWD.

DEAR DICK,

I assure you it pains me intensely

 Your modest request to be forced to refuse ;

But though to assent would rejoice me immensely,

 I'm really in no situation to choose.

To postpone to one's children relations more distant

 Is surely a maxim you wouldn't condemn ;

And my family, Dick ! 'twould be scarcely consistent

 With what I regard as my duty to them.

Then forgive me, old boy, that the claims of my wife
and

 My brats before yours—even *yours*—I must rank ;

So heartily wishing you health and long life and
    A bumper next harvest, yours lovingly,

                                          FRANK.

    DEAR FRANK,

I'm aware of my " once removed " cousins,
    But *I*, recollect, am a " father of five,"
While my tenants, alas ! can display them in dozens,
    A-swarm in their cabins like bees in a hive.

Tim Doolan, with eight, hasn't found it convenient
    To pay me a farthing for two years and more ;
And, in spite of my five, I'm obliged to be lenient,
    So, you, too, might manage it, Frank, with your four.

I think we should help one another to bear it—
    This burden by which the whole country is bowed ;
And I cannot but think you are ready to share it
    With yours very faithfully,

                            DICKY O'DOWD.

DEAR DICK,

You behaved with a wise moderation,
   I own, when your claim on Tim Doolan you sank ;
But I cannot perceive that a like obligation
   Devolves upon yours very faithfully,

FRANK.

DEAR FRANK,

Can't you really ?   'Tis I then who labour
   Beneath moral-optic illusions alone.
But I know that the judge of the case of a neighbour
   Is mighty astute to " distinguish " his own.

Yet allow me to say, your humanity-preachings
   Might well be a little less eager and loud
While you throw the expense of applying its teachings
   On yours unassistedly,

DICKY O'DOWD.

SIR,

I beg to acknowledge your insolent letter,
    But care not its sophistries cheap to expose ;
I'm content to remark that I think it is better
    That this correspondence between us should close.

If you cannot perceive the disparity glaring
    Between the two cases you seek to confuse,
I must leave you alone with your blunder, despairing
    Of bringing you round to more sensible views.

But though I shan't waste my own labour in writing,
    To try and point out the mistake you have made,
I may, by a letter my lawyer's inditing,
    Convince you, perhaps, that I mean to be paid.

I want but my money, and do not intend it
    Grabbed up by a covetous landlord to be,
So a cheque if you please, and the sooner you send it
    The better you'll satisfy

                                F. H. O'D.

Sir,

Take and be—happy, the sum that I owe you,

    The slice from your debtor, you Shylock avowed!

It is something at least and at last that I *know* you.

    Your luckless Antonio,

                  Richard O'Dowd.

Post scriptum.—I erred, and I own it with candour,

    In thinking, misled by analogy loose,

To apply to the humanitarian gander

    Your sauce for the landed-proprietor goose.

THE PUZZLED HISTORIAN.

(1880.)

"WHAT is the drift of it?   Where is the key to it?
  Fog and perplexity!   What does it mean?
Search as I may, no solution I see to it,
  Nowhere the trace of a clue to be seen."

Such is the cry the South African mystery,
  Wrapt as 'twill seem in obscurity dense,
Surely will draw from the writer of history,
  Sifting the matter a century hence.

" Come now, together once more let me pull myself,"
  Thus will he mutter with resolute frown ;
" Else I shall think I am growing as dull myself,
  Dull as the Blue-books I have to boil down.

"Yes! it is clear that a certain Commissioner
　　Occupied (let me be sure of the year—
Seventy-nine) at the Cape the position or
　　Office of ruler—that's perfectly clear.

" Clear it is too (for a scrutiny rigorous
　　Settles the point) that Commissioner Frere
Does, for proceedings imprudently vigorous,
　　Get himself wigged by the Government here.

" Wigged with asperity, wigged with severity
　　(Whigs cannot wig as Conservatives can);
So that one thinks he'll resign with celerity
　　Such as becomes a high-spirited man.

" Ah! but he doesn't; that's quite incontestable;
　　Clearly, yes clearly, he doesn't resign :
Swallows his wigging and finds it digestible,
　　Sticks to his office through Seventy-nine.

" What have we then ?　Why, a furious clamour and
　　Angry demands for Sir Bartle's recall ;
Gladstone—*the* Gladstone—attacking him hammer and
　　Tongs, and protesting the loudest of all !

" Levity, rashness, inordinate vanity,
　　Chauvinist arrogance, stubborn self-will,
Callous contempt for the claims of humanity—
　　Such were the terms of which Frere had his fill.

" Faults intellectual, moral obliquities,
　　Shared, it was said, the Commissioner's mind ;
' Wildest of follies ' or ' worst of iniquities '
　　Equally truly his action defined.

" Thus we go on until changes political
　　Bring to a close the Conservative reign,
Placing this Gladstone—the closest of critical
　　Study assures me—in office again.

" Now then, I thought, 'twill all up with Sir Bartle be,
    Gladstone will have him back home pretty soon ;
Or *he* may think his more dignified part'll be
    That of the Colonel's intelligent 'coon.

" No, not a bit of it ! quite the reverse of it ;
    Colonel and 'coon get on capital terms ;
Federal scheme is revived, and, as nurse of it,
    Frere in his office the Premier confirms.

" Frere, the atrocious, the quite indefensible ;
    Maker of barbarous wars has become
Frere, the sagacious, the quite indispensable
    Man of the policy favoured at home.

" Wonders on wonders ! but by this addition or
    Rather completion the summit is topped ;
Frere, the forgiven and trusted Commissioner,
    Shortly discovers his salary stopped !

"Surely a body of fables incredible
   Gathering round this Commissioner Frere!
One I could swallow, or two might be edible,
   Hardly the whole—in a single career.

" Wigged by Conservative chiefs who appointed him,
   Cursed—and conserved by the Whigs who attacked!
Feathered and tarred by the priests who anointed him,
   Whitewashed by those at whose hands he was
      blacked !

" Sternly rebuked—and with signal humility
   Bowing his head and consenting to stay !
Fiercely reviled—and retained for ability !
   Highly commended—and docked of his pay !

" Have I as one two Commissioners reckoned, or
   Is there a brace of Prime Ministers here?
Are there two Gladstones, a first and a second, or
   Is there, perchance, an alternative Frere ?

" Vainly, ah vainly, I strive with the mystery ;

Vainly I hunt for the clue that I miss ;

Fog and perplexity !   Who would the history

Wish to compose of a people like this ? "

"OUR GLYCERINE BAROMETER."

(1880.)

THE violent storm which is still raging around us has come opportunely to illustrate the significance of the records which we commenced publishing on Monday of the readings of the Jordan Glycerine Barometer recently established at this office.—*The Times,* Oct. 29.

SCENE.—*Editorial Room in Printing-House Square. The Editor of the 'Times' discovered seated at a table. A storm is raging. To him enters a Sub-Editor.*

Recitative.

SUB-EDITOR.

How fiercely chides the storm without,
How howl the winds in devil's din!

And see with news of rack and rout

What telegrams come pouring in !

From Falmouth to the Firth of Tay

Our sea-lashed coasts with wrecks are strewn,

Wind-hunted ships crowd every bay.

ED.

God bless my soul ! how opportune !

SUB-E.

From east to west, from north to south,

The floods are out for miles and miles ;

From watershed to river-mouth

The banks lie hidden (strange ! he smiles)

At Bath a house . . . but how is this ?

You hear with fortitude sublime

These shocking—

ED.   Well, the secret is

They happen in the nick of time.

Air.

THE EDITOR.

Let tempests work their wildest will,
 Let torrent-rain our meadows flood,
Ill were the wind, and worse than ill,
 That blew to no man aught of good.
This hurricane that sweeps the skies,
 One really almost might aver
'Twas sent express to advertise
 Our Glycerine Barometer.

For marked ye not, on Tuesday last,
 When Gordon Bennett flashed " Beware !
A dangerous gale is speeding fast
 Towards your fated shores. Prepare ! "
How in its tube the fluid fell,
 And how the storm which would occur
It did to all the world foretell—
 Our Glycerine Barometer.

So was it published to mankind
   What precious food the 'Times' supplies
To those who seek its page to find
   The wisdom of the weather-wise.
To all the journals of the day
   Such persons should our print prefer,
Since in its office hangs alway
   A Glycerine Barometer.

One column of instructive stuff
   They're sure to find—that one I mean
Which we must now with vigour puff,
   And which consists of Glycerine.
For though our news be somewhat stale,
   And though our views may sometimes err,
Nor novelty nor truth can fail
   Our Glycerine Barometer.

What if a daily hash we make
   Of names, dates, titles, and degrees,

If rank as Colonels Captains take
   And "Barts." descend to K.C.B.'s ?
What if our "reader " takes no heed
   And printers' errors oft recur ?
At least we acurately read
   Our Glycerine Barometer.

What if of news on every lip .
   No notice in the 'Times' appears,
And frightful gas explosions slip
   Unheeded past our dreaming ears ?
At least our vigilance is good
   For signs of atmospheric stir :
No surreptitious storms elude
   Our Glycerine Barometer.

                (A pause.   Then somewhat sadly :)
Yet in my joy—'tis always so—
   A seed of bitterness is hid :
" Leporum fonte medio
   Amari surgit aliquid."

I see, and not without a shock,
New triumphs older glories blur,
And mourn our famous Weathercock
Outshone by our Barometer.

THE FUN OF IT.

(1880.)

"No one gives us any fun." . . . .—*Spectator, Dec.* 11.

'TIS very true, thou thoughtful Print;
 Of that same fun thou hankerest after
There seems just now a certain stint
 In manufactories of laughter.

Yet deem not, good *Spectator*, pray,
 That we poor melancholy creatures
Find not in politics to-day
 Abundance of amusing features.

'Tis funny—every one must own,
 Without distinction, Whig and Tory—
This Ireland paralysed and prone,
 Her neck beneath the foot of Rory.

Droll in themselves her troubles are;
  And judges note at each assizes
Their wealth of incidents *bizarre*,
  Their fruitfulness in quaint surprises.

We all enjoy—as who would not?—
  The " points " in the agrarian battle :
The tenants tortured, landlords shot;
  The tail-docked sheep, the hamstrung cattle ;

The rude art-work of Rory's pen,
  Symbolical of threatened lives;
The graves of yet unmurdered men
  Absurdly dug in carriage-drives.

We mark the comic element
  That visible in Boycott's fate is,
The forty score of troopers sent
  To help get in the Captain's " praties."

We see the joke when pale police
  Entreat a man to curb his anger
And take his cudgelling in peace,
  Or " all their lives" would be in danger.

We feel the humour of reports
  That, where the Queen's writ runs no longer,
There the Land-Leaguers' mimic courts
  (Less learned than "the Four"—but stronger)

Make orders instantly obeyed ;
  Give judgments, unreviewed for error;
And wield, in short, that playful blade,
  The dagger of the Irish Terror.

These things divert ; but underneath
  There lies this piece of broader humour,
That while the patient bleeds to death
  The doctors' strife engrosses Rumour.

Law, Order, Life kept waiting on
  The wrangling, fumbling legislator!
That joke's too plain for mother's son
  To miss, I take it, dear *Spectator*.

So if to laugh we are not quick,
  Although we own the jest so gladly,
Ascribe it to our English trick
  Of taking all our pleasures sadly.

Just so should we, I dare to say,
  In Rome's most famous conflagration,
Have viewed in the same stolid way
  The humours of the situation;

Nor, as we watched the city burn,
  Should we (for man's so strange a riddle)
Have yearned, as you appear to yearn,
  For the brisk notes of Nero's fiddle.

E

"DOWN TO DESSERT."

(1881.)

Non nobis! The dinner is over,
  Speed waiters the table to clear ;
Disappears through the door the last cover—
  But stay ! what new guests have we here ?
Who are these who come wearily trooping—
  A strange unpresentable crowd,
With shoulders ungracefully stooping,
  And knees somewhat awkwardly bowed ;
In whose faces, though lacking in fulness,
  The careful observer descries,
To redeem them from absolute dulness,
  The wolf's* most expressive of eyes ?

The remains of the feast they examine
  With hunger's keen glances alert:
Can it be that these children of Famine
  Are only asked in to dessert ?

Can it be ?   Yes, it certainly can be :
  The host, with magnificent air,
Bids welcome each want-stricken man be,
  And leads him in state to a chair.
" My friends ! " he exclaims with emotion,
  " Your dinner, I fear will be small ;
But, believe me, I hadn't a notion
  You cared about dinners at all.
To forget that extreme inanition
  Disposes a man to a meal
Was—was . . . . well, of course, an omission,
  As now I regretfully feel.
But the moment I heard you'd expected
  Your 'cards' would be sent, and were hurt

At the thought that your claims were neglected

   I asked you at once to dessert.

" But should I keep talking for ever

   The past I should fail to undo ;

So, late being better than never,

   I beg you at once to fall to.

The prime haunch of venison is finished,

   The saddle of mutton all gone,

The baron of beef is diminished

   To yon undesirable bone.

But we've gooseberries crimson and yellow,

   And strawberries (best *without* cream);

Those plums are delightfully mellow,

   Those nuts—though I say it—supreme.

On those olives—best French, I assure you—

   Your powers of consumption exert;

No pains have been spared to procure you

   A truly *recherché* dessert."

Oh, Gladstone ! look well at that table !

    Look well at it, Forster and Bright !

De vobis narratur my fable :

    Can none of you read it aright ?

When the strong meats of land-confiscation

    Were dressed for the peasant's repast,

Was it really humane legislation

    To think of the hungriest last ?

It is not very pleasant perceiving

    That you who that banquet have spread

Could so quietly contemplate leaving

    These poor squalid wretches unfed ;

That the fruits of your cutting and carving

    To tenants alone should revert,

And the labourer, landless and starving,

    Be only " brought down to dessert."

.

THE PATRIARCH'S HOME-COMING.

(1881.)

BEYOND the Vaal, in those wild lands,
　　The " simple scriptural people's " seat,
A farmstead in the gloaming stands
　　Alert its lord's return to greet.

The clean-swept floor, the dusted shelf;
　　The new-lit lamp's expectant look ;
The trim array of shining delf;
　　The arm-chair in the ingle-nook ;

The cosy curtains close drawn in ;
　　The housewife listening at the door
With hand upraised to hush the din
　　Of younker-gambols on the floor ;

All tell a tale of anxious love;
  While, open on the window-seat,
A Bible's well-thumbed pages prove
  Where fears and faith's assurance meet.

But hark! that sound! a horse's neigh,
  The lowing of a startled steer,
The tramp of hoofs upon the way;
  "It is! it is! my Piet is here!"

O sanctity of wife-embrace!
  Let none with supercilious shrug
Deride a simple scriptural race
  Who thus can conjugally hug.

And now when kissed were wife and child
  "Say, Piet, 'tis not bad luck again?"
Cried anxious wife: the husband smiled
  And pointed proudly at his train.

" Look, Vrow ! " he said : and at the view
   She turned, her tears of joy to hide.
" I knew it would be so ! I knew
   The Lord," she murmured, " would provide !

" I prayed ; and waited free from fear
   Till he should bring you back once more
Victorious of your bow and spear,
   Blest in your basket and your store.

" And lo ! He puts some dozen head
   Of noble beasts within your reach,
With many a fine large Kaffir maid
   Well worth at least ten shillings each !

" So now, my Piet, with heartfelt thanks
   Break we the Christian's humble bread :
Tether the cattle in their ranks,
   And put the hussies in the shed ! "

Then they two, with no formal grace,
    But asking, as from hearts that feel,
A benediction, took their place
    Before their frugal evening meal.

And many a sympathetic prayer
    From Radicals beyond the sea
Was breathed above the worthy pair
    And blessed their simple scriptural tea.

THE MODEST POSTULATES.

(1880.)

LET it be granted that mankind
  Put off all passions sinister,
And got a new and virtuous mind
  When we got our new Minister ;

Let it be granted we have found
  That Gladstone's mere arising
The long-divided world has bound
  In brotherhood surprising ;

That Russians from their plots desist,
  And find a solace sweeter
In working out the will of Christ
  Than any Will of Peter ;

That Italy now no longer dreams
   A new Trentine Magenta;
That Austria cares not who redeems
   Italia Irredenta;

That Germany suspects not France,
   That France forgives her neighbour;
And both lead off the Arcadian dance
   With pastoral pipe and tabor;

That men are dragged from plough and desk
   And armed and drilled by millions
Merely to make more picturesque
   Millennial cotillons;

That all the nations, in a word,
   Our Gladstone's visions now share,
And yearn to turn the spear and sword
   To pruning-hook and ploughshare;

That envy, restlessness, and dread,
   And sleepless-eyed suspicion,
And hope, and hate, and greed are dead
   And buried—with ambition;

That no one fears to lose his own,
   Or other's goods has wanted:
Be these our postulates alone;
   Let only these be granted,

And we may sing our Q.E.D.
   With lawful jubilation;
For " Europe's Concert " proved will be
   By force of " demonstration."

WHAT SHALL WE THINK OF THE KURDS?

(1880.)

WORSHIPFUL patrons of " young nationalities,"
 Ardent promoters of " movements of race,"
Learned in Destinies, Forces, Fatalities,
 Help us to settle a troublesome case.
  For proper bestowing
  Of sympathies glowing
We feel a solicitude stronger than words;
  So, please, a suggestion
  For solving the question
Of what should be thought of the Kurds.

How should it act on our moral economy
 Tidings to get of Abdullah the Sheikh

Boldly proclaiming a Kurdish autonomy,

   Just as it might be Slavonic or Greek ?

      This being read of him,

      What's to be said of him—

   He who this national movement has stirred ?

      How should we meet it,

      How properly treat it—

   The raid of this vigorous Kurd ?

Turkey we all of us know is " unspeakable ; "

   Persia is " cruel, corrupt, and effete ; "

Should we, then, hope that Abdullah's a Sheikh able

   Sultan and Shah and their armies to beat ?

      Does he, like Hofer,

      A tyrant to " go for,"

   A sword of deliverance valiantly gird ?

      Ought we to pray for him ?

      Ought we to say for him

Go it, my patriot Kurd ?

Or shall we check sentimental intensities

While we recall the repute of the tribe,

Persons to whom certain ugly propensities

Common report has been wont to ascribe—

A proneness unpleasant

To harry the peasant,

His homestead to wreck and to seize on his herds,

To ravish and slaughter

Wife, grandam, and daughter—

For that is the way of the Kurds ?

Say, shall we then to an infamous State or to

Infamous subjects our favour refuse ?

Answer us, sweet casuistic *Spectator*, do !

Prithee enlighten us, good *Daily News !*

Let us know whether,

Comparing by feather

These most disagreeably similar birds,

Morality's letter

And spirit go better

With blessing or banning the Kurds.

Can we wish well to the cause of autocracy,

    Knowing the sins of the Sultan and Shah ?

Can we for triumph of Kurdish democracy—

    Triumph of murderous brigands—hurrah ?

        Or would it be moral,

        In view of this quarrel,

Impartial dislike to distribute in thirds :

        Two parts of aversion

        For Turk and for Persian,

Remainder reserved for the Kurds ?

A CONGRATULATORY ODE.

(1878.)

[THE *true* version of the congratulatory Latin ode addressed to
the Berlin Congress by "the well-known German poet Gustave
Schwetschke," and "distributed by Prince Bismarck's request
among the Plenipotentiaries"—none other being genuine.]

Rideamus igitur,

Socii Congressus ;

Post dolores bellicosos,

Post labores bumptiosos,

Fit mirandus messus.

Ubi sunt qui apud nos

Lites litigâre,

F

Moldo-Wallachæ frementes,

Græculi esurientes?

Heu! absquatulâre.

Ubi sunt provinciæ

Quas est laus pacâsse?

Totæ, totæ sunt partitæ:

Has tulerunt Muscovitæ,

Illas Count Andrassy.

Et quid est quod Angliæ

Dedit hic Congressus?

Jus pro aliis pugnandi,

Mortuum vivificandi—

Splendidi successus!

Vult Joannes decipi

Et bamboosulatur.

Io Beacche!   Quæ majestas!

Ostreæ reportans testas

Domum gloriatur!

A LITERARY "CAUSE CÉLÈBRE.

(1876.)

[SAMUEL PERKINS *expoundeth the moral thereof to his son*, DUDLEY JAMES PERKINS.]

HERE he comes! The paper, Mary. Ah, good morn-
ing, Dudley James.

'Ave you read this libel haction—this 'ere case of—
what's their names?

Oh, Buchanan *vussus* Taylor—there's a lesson, lad,
for you

In them singerlar proceedins; take and read 'em,
Dudley, do.

You who've caused so much disquiet both to me and
to your ma,

Not to say your aunt Jemima, where your expectations are.

Yes, you know you 'ave, my boy; it's gettin' on for
  nigh a year

Since you took to dress in velvet and knocked off
  your dinner-beer,

Took to wear your collars lower and asoomed a moody
  stare;

'Ad a row with Snipp's assistant when he come to cut
  your 'air;

Took to moonin' round the counter, muttrin' "lines
  to" doose knows what,

Hodes and sonnicks, songs and ballids—and the other
  rhymin' rot;

Changed your short black cutty for a dangling
  German chaney pipe

And refused to join the fam'ly at the evenin' meal
  of tripe;

Wouldn't take your ma o' Sundays to the "Welsh
  Harp" in the shay,

But remained at home to finish your "Romaunt of
  Pegwell Bay."

Yes, my laddie, I have watched you—I have seen
    your little game,

I've observed your haspirations after a poetic
    fame—

"Fame himmortal," if you please—for nothing short
    of that will do.

Trade is low and butter vulgar—poetry's the line
    for you !

Now, my boy, just read that haction—that'll tell
    you what they are,

These 'ere poets that are soarin' o'er our 'eads so
    jolly far.

Parts of it I 'ardly follered, but its English seems
    to be,

Messrs Swinbun and Buchanan can't agree to dis-
    agree.

Mr B. he wrote a satter, — droppin' down on
    Mr S.,

And complainin' as his werses were a little too
    "undress."

Well, this put, you may imagine, Mr S. upon his
    mettle.

"What! you call my werse indecent? Gammon! it's
    the pot and kettle."

So he ups and slates Buchanan, calls him all the
    'orrid names

He can take and lay his tongue to—which is plenty,
    Dudley James—

Treats the hother as a hinsect, looked at thro' the
    microscope

By a far superior being — which is funny, let us
    'ope.

That, of course, annoys Buchanan, and he " counters "
    with a will,

Calling Mr S. a "monkey "—which, let's 'ope, is
    funnier still.

Then they drops it for a season (this occurred in
    '71).

But you don't know much of poets if you think the
    war was done.

Last year comes out "Jonas Fisher," pokin' up the
"Fleshly School"

Once again: "Oho!" says Swinbun, keepin' very calm
and cool,

"Here's that hodious Buchanan at his dirty game
again

Sure as death. There can't be no one else among
the race of men

Who could think my werse indecent." So he lets
him 'ave it 'ot;

Shied the mud he'd shied before, and shied some more
that he had not.

When Buchanan's all bespattered, then—most 'orrible
of sells—

Lo be'old yer! "Jonas Fisher" proves to be by
summun else.

'Ence the haction which that plucky Mr Peter Taylor
fights.

That you see's what comes of printin' what a hangry
poet writes.

Lor! what larks to see them lawyers overaul Buch-
    anan's lines,

Dippin' in their scoops to try 'em like my cheeses,
    through the rines!

Tastin' this and smellin' t'other. "Isn't this a little
    strong?"

"Call that pure?" "Well, what of this now, for a
    hammatory song?"

Yes, by George, I never laughed so 'earty, nor I never
    shall,

As at earin' Mr 'Awkins read about that Injin
    gal,

And the cuddlin' in the forest! Well, per'aps it
    meant no harm,

Still the author owned hisself the scene was just a
    trifle warm.

Then, of course, Buchanan's counsel—he was not a-
    goin' to fail;

So he dropped upon the "fleshlies" right and left and
    tooth and nail!

"Grossly senshal," "most indecent," "hanimal passion consecrated."

Says the judge, "A style of poitry 'ighly to be de-
precated!"

Well, the upshot was Buchanan gets his verdict safe
and sound,

And he comes on Mr Taylor for a hundern-fifty
pound.

But, Lord love you, my dear Dudley, what a foolish
price to pay!

What a terrible exposy for the poets of the
day!

I dun know about their poems, which is dirty, which
is clean;

As to Mr Swinbun's "Ballids"—blowed if I know
what they mean!

So I gev my Jane a copy on her birthday last
July

Bound as natty as you please in blue morocker—
for, says I,

If my gal finds *them* corruptin', as some people says
they are,

She's a doosed sight more 'andy guessin' riddles than
her Pa!

But to think of them two poets showin' up each
other's lines

For the benefit of us the—what d'you call it?—
Philistines.

Passion, fancy, light and sweetness — well, maybe
they've got 'em all;

But they've one thing undeweloped — gumption:
that's uncommon small!

Why, when Briggs in hopen westry cheeked me—
you remember, Dud,

Makin' insolent allusions to my butter as Thames
mud—

Did I go to lawr about it—hugly-tempered as I
am?

Did I sue old Briggs for libel, defamation?   Not for
Sam!

No, I knew old Briggs's counsel—he'd contrive to
    'ave his fling,

And my butter—well mud's 'umbug, but — *'taint*
    always quite the thing!

And although I know a thing or two about old
    Briggs's tea,

" Boshy butter" don't get nicer by denouncin' " dirt-
    Bohea."

What's the good of each exposin' t'other's tricks of
    trade on hoath?

Plaintiff wins, or p'raps defendant, but the neighbours
    laugh at both;

Yet you find the "'igher intlek" blind to facs as
    plain as this—

Facs which any common tradesman's too much com-
    mon-sense to miss.

Yes, my boy, this ought to cure you—reverations such
    as these.

You will stick to butter, Dudley—butter, bacon, heggs,
    and cheese,

Rather than become a poet like them two as lately
    fought,

Bringin' out their little wash-tubs, stupid-like, in
    hopen court ;

And—to dab each other's faces with the soapy froth
    and foam—

Washed their dirty clothes in public, which they
    might have washed at 'ome !

MIMICRIES

THE GOD AND THE DAMOSEL.

[Suggested by the immortal picture, under this title, of
Mr Symphony Priggins.]

THE GOD.

LOOK in my face, and know me who I am.
I smite and save; I bless, and, lo, I damn.
    Incline thine head, thy browless brow incline;
I touch thee, and I tap thee, and proclaim,
    For ever and for ever thou art mine!

O long as grief, and leaner than desire!
    O sweet retreating breasts and amorous - kissing
        knees!
O grace and goodliness of strait attire! ·
    A robe of them who sport in summer seas.

By these, and by the eyelids of thine eyes,

Ringed round with darkness, swollen weeper-wise,

    By these I know thee ; these are for a sign,

Surer, yea, even than thy most splendid size

    Of spreaden hands : I know thee, thou art mine.

The Damosel.

Master and lord, I know thee who thou art ;

Lo, and with homage of the stricken heart,

    I hail thee, I adore thee, and obtest :

I am thine own, I know no better part ;

    Do with me, master as thee seemeth best.

O loose as thought and bodiless as a dream !

    O globular grand eyes, a bane of maidenhood !

O miracle of tunic-folds that seem

    Self-balanced, firm, a glory of carven wood.

By these, and by the crown thy temples wear,

Holy, a cauline flower of wondrous hair ;

    By thy red mouth, a bow without a chord,

And shaftless, yea, but deadly, O most fair.

I knew thee, and I know thee for my lord!

THE GOD.

Ay, now the flicker of a nauseate smile

Bestirs thy cheek and wan lips imbecile;

Thy pale plucked blossom droops; its day is done.

THE DAMOSEL.

Nay, let me deck my bosom therewithal,

It were ill-ominous to let it fall,

The faithful mistress of Hyperion Sun.

THE GOD.

Stoop thou—what ails thee, child, to shudder?—stoop
and brush

Hair with tow-towzled hair, that for a space

I breathe my godhead through thy thirsting veins, and
flush

The soft submalar hollows of thy face,

G

And thrill thee, crown to sole, till that in downward
    rush
Of eager ecstasy with fair flat feet thou crush
    The beetle, Virtue, in the lowly place.

The Damosel.

Ah, master and lord, I feel it; the wind of thy fierce
    delight,
    Hell-hot as the blast from the furnace, sea-cold as a
        gust of the sea.
O deaf blind Love, that art deaf as a poker and blind
    as the night!
    O my flushed faint cheeks and my chin!   O mine
        eye and the elbow of me !

I bow to thy might, O my lord, to the keen-blown
    breath of thy lips,
    With a loathing of love that longs, and a longing of
        love that loathes,

With shiver of angular shoulders, and shake of invisi-
ble hips,
As boweth the light slight stake in the torture of
wind-whirled clothes!

Thou hast rent me enough, O Divine! . . . and behold,
thou stayest thine hand,
And leavest me crushed as a reed, that I wot not
whether I tread
Upon Earth, our holy old mother, with feet down-
pressing, or stand
Inverse in a fearless new fashion, uplift on my
passionate head!

FROM "THE PUSS AND THE BOOTS."

Put case I circumvent and kill him : good.

Good riddance—wipes at least from book o' th' world

One ugly admiration-note-like blot—

Gives honesty more elbow-room by just

The three dimensions of one wicked knave.

But then slips in the plaguy After-voice.

" Wicked ?   Holloa ! my friend, whither away

So fast ?   Who made you, Moses-like, a judge

And ruler over men to spare or slay ?

A blot wiped off forsooth !   Produce forthwith

Credentials of your mission to erase

The ink-spots of mankind—t' abolish ill

For being what it is, is bound to be,

Its nature being so—cut wizards off

In flower of their necromantic lives
For being wizards, when 'tis plain enough
That they have no more wrought their wizardship
Than cats their cathood." Thus the plaguy Voice,
Puzzling withal not overmuch, for thus
I turn the enemy's flank : " Meseems, my friend,
Your argument's a thought too fine of mesh,
And catches what you would not. Every mouse
Trapped i' the larder by the kitchen wench
Might reason so—but scarcely with effect.
Methinks 'twould little serve the captured thief
To plead, ' The fault's Dame Nature's, guiltless I.
Am I to blame that in the parcelling-out
Of my ingredients the Great Chemist set
Just so much here, there so much, and no more
(Since 'tis but question, after all is said,
Of mere proportion 'twixt the part that feels
And that which guides), so much proclivity
To nightly cupboard-breaking, so much lust
Of bacon-scraps, such tendency to think

Old Stilton-rind the noblest thing on earth?

Then the *per contra*—so much power to choose

The right and shun the wrong; so much of force

Of uncorrupted will to stoutly bar

The sensory inlets of the murine soul,

And, when by night the floating rare-bit fume

Lures like a siren's song, stop nostrils fast

With more than Odusseian sailor-wax :

Lastly so much of wholesome fear of trap

To keep self-abnegation sweet.   Then comes

The hour of trial, when lo ! the suadent scale

Sinks instant, the deterrent kicks the beam,

The heavier falls, the lighter mounts (as much

A thing of law with motives as with plums),

And I, forsooth, must die simply because

Dame Nature, having chosen so to load

The dishes, did not choose suspend for me

The gravitation of the moral world.'

How would the kitchen-wench reply ?   Why thus

(If given, as scullions use, to logic-fence

And keen retorsion of dilemmata

In speeches of a hundred lines or so):

'Grant your plea valid.   Good.   There's mine to hear.

'Twas Nature made you? well: and me, no less;

You she by forces past your own control

Made a cheese-stealer?   Be it so: of me

By forces as resistless and her own

She made a mouse-killer.   Thus, either plays

A *rôle* in no wise chosen of himself,

But takes what part the great Stage Manager

Cast him for, when the play was set afoot.

Remains we act ours—without private spite,

But still with spirit and fidelity,

As fits good actors: you I blame no whit

For nibbling cheese—simply I throw you down

Unblamed—nay, even morally assoiled,

To pussy there: blame thou not me for that.'

Or say perhaps the girl is slow of wit,

Something inapt at ethics—why, then thus:

'Enough of prating, little thief!   This talk

Of "fate, free-will, foreknowledge absolute,"

Is hugely out of place!   What next indeed,

If all the casuistry of the schools

Be prayed in aid by every pilfering mouse

That's caught i' th' trap?   See here, my thieving friend,

Thus I resolve the problem.   We prefer

To keep our cheeses for our own behoof,

And eat them with our proper jaws ; and so,

Having command of mouse-traps, we will catch

Whatever mice we can, and promptly kill

Whatever mice we catch.   *Entendez-vous ?*

Ay, and we *will*, though all the mice on earth

Pass indignation votes, obtest the faith

Of gods and men, and make the welkin ring

With world-resounding dissonance of squeak ! ' "

But hist ! here comes my wizard !   Ready then

My nerves—and talons—for the trial of strength !

A stout heart, feline cunning, and—who knows ?

THE MODERN POET'S SONG.

WHERE hast thou been since battlemented Troy
  Rose like a dream to thy loud-stricken lyre?
    Why dost thou walk the common earth no more?
  Nor lead on high Parnass the Muses' choir,
    As when thy Hellas rang from shore to shore
With harpings loud, and hymns of holy joy?
Well may we for thy gracious presence long:
  The fashion of the day is classic myth,
  And he must liberally deal therewith
Who fain would sing the modern poet's song.

Shake from thy brow the hyacinthine locks
  That hide its ivory splendours! Let thine eyes
    Flash forth as blue-white lightnings lubricate,

Spread sudden day through purple midnight skies,
    Or scarlet shafts of dawn illuminate
The grey and umber of the sleeping rocks!
O colours and O shades of every hue,
    Plain or in combination, faint or strong,
Red, green, and yellow, black and white and blue,
    How ye assist the modern poet's song!

Far-darting Phoibos, lofty Loxias
    (Since thou the glad Greek greeting well mayst
        hear
    That hailed thee erst in Delos the divine),
  If our late lays have leave to reach thine ear,
Meek, myrtle-bearing, give us grace to pass
    Through the white worshippers towards thy shrine.
O apt alliteration! how a throng
    Of self-repeating vowels and consonants,
    How lines of labials, strings of sibilants,
Make music in the modern poet's song!

I will compare thee to a fowler wight,
   Snaring the soul with magic-woven words
     Of wondrous music and divinest art ;
Or haply I may liken, heard aright,
   Thy wingèd strains themselves to captured birds,
     Fast in the meshes of the human heart.
For men and things resemble what we please,
   Such arbitrary powers to bards belong ;
And, in default of genuine similes,
   Conceits will serve the modern poet's song.

Come thou, our lord ; the heart within us dies,
   And, faint as in a breathless land and bare,
     We take no profit of our piteous day.
Give us to look upon thee, O most fair ;
Appear, O sweet desire of all men's eyes,
     Ere this dread cup of life shall pass away !
For vague appeals which we interpret not,
   And moody murmurs at unstated wrong,
And aspirations for we say not what,
   Largely compose the modern poet's song.

Come thou, and I my stanzas will illume

    With all the hues that in the rainbow meet,

    Alliterate all letters that there are ;

Outdo all rivals in mysterious gloom,

    Fetch metaphors like magi from afar,

    Lit by no star of meaning, to thy feet.

For these and similar poetic tricks

    Are highly prized our master's school among.

O Swinburne ! and O water ! how ye mix,

    To constitute the modern poet's song !

AFTER DILETTANTE CONCETTI.

" WHY do you wear your hair like a man,

      Sister Helen ?

This week is the third since you began."

" I'm writing a ballad ; be still if you can,

      Little brother.

     (O Mother Carey, mother !

What chickens are these between sea and heaven ?)"

" But why does your figure appear so lean,

      Sister Helen ?

And why do you dress in sage, sage green ? "

" Children should never be heard, if seen,

      Little brother ?

     (O Mother Carey, mother !

What fowls are a-wing in the stormy heaven !)"

" But why is your face so yellowy white,

> Sister Helen ?

And why are your skirts so funnily tight ? "
" Be quiet, you torment, or how can I write,

> Little brother ?

> *(O Mother Carey, mother !*
How gathers thy train to the sea from the heaven !)"

" And who's Mother Carey, and what is her train,

> Sister Helen ?

And why do you call her again and again ? "
" You troublesome boy, why that's the refrain,

> Little brother.

> *(O Mother Carey, mother !*
What work is toward in the startled heaven ?)"

" And what's a refrain ?   What a curious word,

> Sister Helen !

Is the ballad you're writing about a sea-bird ? "
" Not at all ; why should it be ?   Don't be absurd,

Little brother.

(O Mother Carey, mother !
Thy brood flies lower as lowers the heaven.)"

(A big brother speaketh :)
" The refrain you've studied a meaning had,

Sister Helen !

It gave strange force to a weird ballàd.
But refrains have become a ridiculous 'fad'

Little brother.

And *Mother Carey, mother,*

Has a bearing on nothing in earth or heaven.

" But the finical fashion has had its day,

Sister Helen.

And let's try in the style of a different lay
To bid it adieu in poetical way,

Little brother.

So, Mother Carey, mother !

Collect your chickens and go to—heaven."

(A pause.　Then the big brother sing-
eth, accompanying himself in a plain-
tive wise on the triangle :)

" Look in my face.　My name is Used-to-was ;
I am also called Played-out and Done-to-death,
And It-will-wash-no-more.　Awakeneth
Slowly, but sure awakening it has,
The common-sense of man ; and I, alas !
The ballad-burden trick, now known too well,
Am turned to scorn, and grown contemptible—
A too transparent artifice to pass.

" What a cheap dodge I am !　The cats who dart
Tin-kettled through the streets in wild surprise
Assail judicious ears not otherwise ;
And yet no critics praise the urchin's ' art,'
Who to the wretched creature's caudal part
Its foolish empty-jingling ' burden ' ties."

A DRAWING-ROOM BALLAD.

CAN you recall an ode to June
    Or lines to any river
In which you do not meet the " moon,"
    And see " the moonbeams quiver " ?
I've heard such songs to many a tune,
    But never yet—no niver—
Have I escaped that rhyme to " June "
    Or missed that rhyme to " river."

At times the bard from his refrain
    A moment's respite snatches,
The while his over-cudgelled brain
    At some new jingle catches ;

H

Yet long from the unlucky moon
　　Himself he cannot sever,
But grasps once more that rhyme to " June,"
　　And seeks a rhyme to " river."

Then let not indolence be blamed
　　On him whose verses show it
By shunning " burdens " (rightly named
　　For reader and for poet);
For rhymes must fail him late or soon,
　　Nor can he deal for ever
In words whose sound resembles " June,"
　　And assonants of " river."

When " loon " 's been used, and " shoon " and
　　" spoon,"
　　And " stīver " sounded " stĭver,"
Think of a bard reduced to " 'coon,"
　　And left alone with " liver " !

Ah, then, how blessèd were the boon !
  How doubly blest the giver,
Who gave him one rhyme more for " June,"
  And one more rhyme for " river " !

VERS DE SOCIÉTÉ.

THERE, pay it, James! 'tis cheaply earned ;
   My conscience! how one's cabman charges!
But never mind, so I'm returned
   Safe to my native street of Clarges.
I've just an hour for one cigar
   (What style these Reinas have, and *what* ash!)
One hour to watch the evening star
   With just one Curaçao-and-potash.

Ah me! that face beneath the leaves
   And blossoms of its piquant bonnet!
Who would have thought that forty thieves
   Of years had laid their fingers on it!

Could you have managed to enchant
    At Lord's to-day old lovers simple,
Had Robber Time not played gallant,
    And spared you every youthful dimple !

That Robber bold, like courtier Claude,
    Who danced the gay coranto jesting,
By your bright beauty charmed and awed,
    Has bowed and passed you unmolesting.
No feet of many-wintered crows
    Have traced about your eyes a wrinkle ;
Your sunny hair has thawed the snows
    That other heads with silver sprinkle.

I wonder if that pair of gloves
    I won of you you'll ever pay me !
I wonder if our early loves
    Were wise or foolish, cousin Amy ?

I wonder if our childish tiff

   Now seems to you, like me, a blunder!

I wonder if you wonder if

   I ever wonder if you wonder

I wonder if you'd think it bliss

   Once more to be the fashion's leader!

I wonder if the trick of this

   Escapes the unsuspecting reader!

And as for him who does or can

   Delight in it, I wonder whether

He knows that almost any man

   Could reel it off by yards together!

I wonder if—— What's that? A knock?

   Is that you, James? Eh? What? God bless

     me!

How time has flown! It's eight o'clock,

   And here's my fellow come to dress me.

Be quick, or I shall be the guest
 Whom Lady Mary never pardons;
I trust you, James, to do your best
 To save the soup at Grosvenor Gardens.

POST LUSUS SERIA

TO A FAMOUS PARLIAMENT.

Hunc neque dira venena nec hosticus auferet ensis
Nec laterum dolor aut tussis nec tarda podagra ;
Garrulus hunc quando consumet cumque ; loquace
Si sapiat, vitet, simul atque adoleverit ætas.

As one who from the glacier past the vine
Follows the slow debasement of the Rhine
To where its foiled and sluggish waters creep
Through sand-obstructed channels to the deep—
As such an one may in fantastic mood
Muse on the checkered fortunes of the flood,
The source majestic whence its streams descend,
Its proud career and its ignoble end,—
Thus—but in sober earnestness—are we,
O English Parliament, to think of thee ?

Of thee on flats of dull Obstruction found

The long-descended and the high-renowned!

O thou whose shame or glory is our own,

Born with our birth, and with our growth upgrown!

Was it for this the wasting hand of time,

Perils of youth, and maladies of prime,

Spared thee so long?   O thou who first didst draw

In a rude age the infant breath of law,

And, storing silent increments of life

Through our long era of dynastic strife,

Take gradual heart of grace thy voice to raise

From whispering humbleness of Tudor days;

Wrest the high sceptre from thy Stuart lords;

Bend only for an hour to Cromwell's swords;

Live faction down, break through corruption's chains,

And of the Walpole-poison purge thy veins;

Wax stronger and still stronger, till the land

Saw all its forces gathered to thine hand—

Didst thou thus triumph that thou thus shouldst fall?

Is that proud head that towers over all

Destined to bow before unworthy foes?

Had ever splendid life so mean a close

As thine will show, if thou, for all thy past,

Must die of talk and Irishmen at last?

ON A FAMOUS BILL: THE LAWYER'S SOLILOQUY.

I HOLD it clear, as one who sings
    The party song in divers tones,
    That men may rise on stepping-stones
Of brazen speech to higher things.

And, holding this as maxim chief,
    Ill were my part of lawyer played
    Did I not welcome undismayed
The burden of this desperate brief.

For well his trade he understood,
    And wise that statesman was, I wot,
    Who valued their assistance not
That helped him when his case was good:

Who knew how cheaply could be had
   The summer-weather partisan,
   And used to say, " Give *me* the man
That backs me when my case is bad ! "

I am that man.   Behold in me
   A faithful yeoman of debate,
   Ever at hand the case to state
For Land Bill Number Twenty-three.

O Bill, unfriended of the wise,
   Poor derelict of truth and sense,
   Thy blackest blot and worst offence
Is light and virtue in my eyes.

They say thy purpose is concealed,
   And that the coy design which strays
   Nymph-like, through tangled woods of phrase
Might blush to find itself revealed.

The more the need that I should spare
  No pains to lead the chase awry,
  The while I vigorously cry,
" The nymph, although unseen, is fair ! "

The dull Economist fulfils
  His mission to denounce thy scheme
  As flattery of the peasant's dream
And worsening of his waking ills.

The greater the demand on me
  For cheaply manufactured sneers
  At imbeciles who feed their fears
On bugbears of Economy.

Of contracts' broken faith they prate,
  Of justice made a Lesbian rule,
  And law degraded to the tool
Of mean expediencies of State.

And here they touch me nearly—here
  They press me home : yet only so
  Can all the party zeal I show
Clothed in its full deserts appear.

So much the greater shall my feat
  Of bold apostasy be found,
  So louder shall my praises sound
Where Tadpoles and where Tapers meet,

In that I falter not nor swerve
  From Ministerial paths, nor err
  Through foolish reverence for Her
Whose bread I eat, whose shrine I serve :

That, holding Justice not in awe,
  I find no filial wrath upflame
  Though bastard legislation shame
The household of her priestess, Law ;

I

But bear to see her bed defiled—
　Nay, dare, unnaturally brave,
　To strike my mother dead to save
Blind Faction's misbegotten child !

AVE CÆSAR! MORTUI TE SALUTANT.

(*June* 1879.)

"Yes, it is well to mourn him," foes
    Alike with friends can say;
That bright young life's pathetic close
    Disarms all hates to-day.

None needs to grudge that there be flung
    On that untimely grave
All flowers of pity for the young,
    The innocent, the brave.

Not his the sins that marred his land,
    Though they were sinned for him;
No war was kindled by *his* hand
    Because his star grew dim.

And therefore it is well that now
　　The willing tear be shed
For the poor stripling Prince laid low
　　Among inglorious dead.

But also well that we should mark
　　Hovering above the gate
Of death, the levelled hand, the dark
　　And awful brows of Fate ;

And hear what ghostly murmurs swell
　　Around the fatal spot,
From countless shades of those who fell
　　At Wörth and Gravelotte.

" What robe of empire now clothes on
　　This body pierced and bare ?
Where is the purple, Cæsar's son,
　　We died that you might wear ?

Was it for this we shed our blood,
   For this poor naked prey
Of savage wile, this fated food
   For Zulu assegai?

Left we for this our children dear,
   Sweet faces of our wives?
Cæsar—if Death the dead can hear—
   Give back to us our lives!"

THE AGE OF DESPAIR.

" DRINK deep of life ere death's unending calm
Enfold thee round."   So runs the dreary psalm,
   Miscalled a song of joy, by poets sung,
From jesting Horace down to grave Khayyam.

We sing it now; but who that sings achieves
One hour's pure triumph over him who grieves?
   Who can rejoice in summer, if his heart
Fore-hear the rustle of the falling leaves?

Vainly the farce of gaiety is played;
Death smiles sardonic on the poor parade;
   Nor can our hollow laughters exorcise
That spectre whom the old-world revellers laid.

The rose they wreathed around the careless head,
The wine they poured, the perfumes that they shed,
   The eyes that smiled on them, the lips they pressed,
For *us* what are they?   Faded, vapid, dead!

Dead is for us the rose we know must die;
Long ere we drain the goblet it is dry;
   And, even as we kiss, the distant grave
Chills the warm lip and dims the lustrous eye!

Too far our race has journeyed from its birth;
Too far Death casts his shadow o'er the earth.
   Ah! what remains to strengthen and support
Our hearts, since they have lost the trick of mirth,

The stay of fortitude?   The lofty pride
Wherewith the sages of the Porch denied
   That pain and death are evils, and proclaimed
Lawful the exit of the suicide?

Alas, not so !   No Stoic calm is ours ;
We dread the thorns who joy not in the flowers.
   We dare not breathe the mountain-air of Pain,
Droop as we may in Pleasure's stifling bowers.

What profits it, if here and there we see
A spirit nerved by trust in God's decree,
   Who fronts the grave in firmness of the faith
Taught by the Carpenter of Galilee ?

Who needs not wine nor roses, lute nor lyre,
Scorns life, or quits it by the gate of fire,
   Erect and fearless—what is that to us
Who hold him for the dupe of vain desire ?

Can we who wake enjoy the dreamer's dream ?
Will the parched treeless waste less hideous seem
   Because there shines before some foolish eyes
Mirage of waving wood and silver stream ?

Ah, miserable race! Too weak to bear,
Too sad for mirth, too sceptical for prayer!
  Surely on you the Scripture is fulfilled,
To bid the mountains cover your despair!

THE ANTS' NEST

THE ANTS' NEST.

I'VE an ants' nest in my garden, and on sleepy summer
   days
I delight to sit beside it, and to watch the works and
   ways
Of the busy little people (watched of late too closely
   these
By a far less kindly Virgil than who sang the civic
   bees),
While I muse upon the impulse, silent, hidden—full
   of awe,
Whether it be force of Godhead or of self-fulfilling
   law,—
That, by every year's mid-season, crowds the air with
   humming wings,
Covers earth's abounding bosom with the toil of tiny
   things.

Thus engaged the other evening, lounged me by my
    gardener's boy,

Futile lout and turnip-headed, whom I foolishly
    employ

At a certain weekly stipend to do nothing with a
    hoe,

And to train the climbing roses where I want them
    not to grow :

Lounged me by, I say, this booby, and, in passing—
    Master Sam

Being of the age when mischief has the zest of
    epigram—

Poised a heavy hob-nailed Blucher o'er the hapless
    little state,

And with one strong kick of ruin spurned it flat and
    desolate !

Thus he did. Then I, indignant at the blockhead's
    brutal jest,

Seized him by the nape, and straightway to his ample
    ears addressed,

In the only way to make them take a message to his
    brain,

Strong advice against indulging in such pleasantries
    again.

Off he sneaked, *demissâ caudâ*, and I turned me, full
    of ruth,

To the commonwealth subverted by the too facetious
    youth,

Seeking if, among the ruins of their city thus laid
    low,

Haply might be found a suburb still inhabitable.
    No !

Thread-like street and atom gateway, where awhile
    ago had trod

Tiny feet of thronging thousands, all was formless
    mould and clod ;

Only here and there were hurrying houseless burghers
    two or three,

Dazed, bewildered, void of counsel, o'er the hideous
    débris,

Waiting doubtless *his* appearing, calm amid their
    shattered haunts,

His, the shepherd of the people, his, the "leader
    born of ants,"

The creative, the constructive, "still, strong" ant,
    with purpose high

Order to educe from chaos, law evoke from anarchy;

Who shall nerve his helpless fellows with their ad-
    verse fates to cope,

Fortify them with his patience, animate them with his
    hope;

So that, howsoever slowly, with whatever toil and pain,

From its ruins may the devastated city rise again,

And resume its peaceful labours and renew its pros-
    perous day

Unmolested—till some other booby chance to pass
    that way.

Moralising o'er my claret in my library that night,

" Ah!" thought I, " how much more hopeful, arduous
    though it be, the fight

Fought by man with hostile Nature's banded forces,
    age by age,

Than is waged by lower races, or than they can ever
    wage!

Yonder ants repair their ruins: well, a city straight
    appears

Built as ants have built their cities any time these
    myriad years;

Just as fragile and defenceless, nowise safer in the
    least,

From the boot of playful boyhood, or the hoof of
    straying beast.

Weak they stand, and fall through weakness, and in
    weakness rise again,

Death instructs not, and disaster brings not wisdom
    in its train.

But mankind? We stand confronting calm our over-
    shadowing foe,

Lightnings strike us, tempests whelm us, plague and
    famine lay us low;

K

Yet with every blow he levels weaker grows the giant
blind,

Stronger Polypheme's Odysseus foreordained — the
human mind;

Stronger grows man's strength of cunning his world-
enemies to brave,

Some to baffle, some to conquer, some to capture and
enslave.

Fire he tames, and water serves him, earth her treas-
ure-hiding robe

Raises at his bidding, lightning speeds his message
round the globe.

These once foes he makes his vassals; other foes more
hostile still,

Irreclaimable to service, forces only strong for
ill,

These he cheats or neutralises, circumvents or turns
aside,

Ever setting back their limits as sea-walls set back
the tide.

Each succeeding generation breathes a stronger health-
    ier breath ;

Every decade sees new tillage conquered from the
    wastes of death ;

Nature yearly makes submissions ; soon the philo-
    sophic dream

Will become the workday waking, and mankind will
    reign supreme,

Master of the world around him, king of his environ-
    ment

Absolute, and waiting only that deliverance latest-
    sent,

Man's redemption from his passions, from that scourge
    self-wielded, crime,

From the brutal lust of battle (blunted even now by
    time),

And from competition, blindest of the conflicts that
    divide

And dividing weaken workers who should labour side
    by side—

Which deliverance once accomplished, dawns for him
a brighter day

Than the golden age of fable, never more to pass
away!

Shall we then," I cried elated (reaching down from off
its shelf

'Comte,' in Martineau's translation), "shall we only
live for self?

We of the unbounded future shall we in the present
rest,

Narrowing ant-like aspirations to the limits of our
nest;

Striving through life's summer only as the ant labori-
ous strives

To provide what may suffice us for the winter of our
lives?

And not rather learn to look beyond our own day's
little span,

So to live that we may help to hasten on the Reign of
Man.

Forasmuch as surely knowing, while we labour and
    abstain,
That our labour in our Lord, Humanity, is not in
    vain."

How it chanced I do not know—
That my claret served me so,
Sound as is that modest drink,
I am loath indeed to think ;
But howbeit, truth to tell,
Musing thus asleep I fell,
And I heard a Voice whose tones
Froze the marrow in my bones,
Crying, " Labour and abstain !
Labour spent will not be vain
If it harden thee to bear
The full weight of man's despair :
And to practise abstinence
From the pleasant things of sense,

Easier makes of abnegation
Pleasures of imagination."
Here a pause; then once again:
"Labour, labour, and abstain,
Ye who will—or ye who can,
But ere thou, O dreamer Man,
Take the altruistic vow,
Pledge thy comfortable Now
To insure a glorious Then
To the common race of men,
Open eyes of sleep and see
 What the womb of time is bearing,
 What millennium is preparing
For 'your Lord' Humanity."

The voice surceased: and in a hush of awe
 The walls of dark were riven, and the night
Became as day around me, and I saw,
 As from a tower, a strange and fearful sight.

Earth, kindly Earth, our blithe and blossoming home,
   Far as to where her limits seemed to meet
A sky spread o'er her like an iron dome,
   Lay dead beneath my feet !

Dead—or her only life, the life-in-death
   Of moss and lichen; mute, with such repose
As stirs but when the iceberg sundereth,
   Or sounds the distant grinding of the floes.

This earth of springs and harvests, flocks and herds,
   Of toiling, laughing, loving, human throngs;
Warmed by the sun, and glad with flight of birds,
   And rained on by their songs,

      .

Lay fruitless, soundless, dead: from zone to zone
   Spread over her the terrible control
Of Arctic frost—the idle gloom, the lone
   And everlasting leisure of the Pole !

Spake again the Voice abhorred :
" Lo, the kingdom of your Lord !
Lo, his dazzling palace-walls,
And the silence in his halls,
Marking in its depth intense
A profounder reverence
Than abates the courtier's tones
At the foot of lower thrones.—
Idle dreamer ! vain and blind !
Had thy vision-ridden mind
In its scheme of earthly bliss
And dominion room for *this ?*
Didst thou think that taming these,
Lightning, famine, fire, disease—
Powers that take thy yoke, or flee
From thy face—was conquering Me ?
Fool of foolish boastings !   They
Are my children at their play !
What so wastes the face of earth
Is but malice of their mirth ;

All your famous victories gained

Mean but infants' sports restrained.

Deeper for your real foe

Search ye—I abide below,

Storing for your ' age of gold '

Treasure of eternal cold,

Weaving for man's ' majesty '—

Him, whose expectations high

All your toils and hopes absorb

On this slowly-freezing orb—

Such a robe as may be meet

For—a monarch's winding-sheet."

" Then is He the Creator of things ? or is It their voli-

tionless cause,

Is it Spirit or Force," I cried, in a passion of won-

der and woe,

" That breathes free life out of freedom, or, binding,

is bound by laws ?

Was it choice or chance—was it Demon or Demi-
    urge ordered it so ?

" Is our master a sightless Strength, unwilled—our
    oppressor in chains
  Of the iron he lays on ourselves ? it is well : we can
    learn to bear
As the slaves of a slave endure, for whom in their
    cruellest pains
  No longings of unwreaked hate disturb the content
    of despair.

" But a Person ?   A Cause Uncaused ?   Can it be
    that deliberate Will,
  At a point in the vast Before whereunto no mind
    can climb,
Appointed such end and prepared it, selecting such
    means to fulfil,
  Or e'er from Eternity's ocean arose the island of
    Time ?

"Can it be that the planets obeyed a commanding
    Voice? Can it be
That no aimless impulse arrayed them around the
    solar fire,
But that floatings of nebular masses were changed by
    conscious decree
To the rhythmical music and march of a solid and
    orderly choir?

"That the first faint thrills of the germ and the blind
    beginnings of life
Were marked by a sentient Mind that, of fixed pre-
    determinate plan,
Had willed the fierce struggle of living, the pitiless
    secular strife,
And thereout in the fulness of untold years the
    emergence of Man;

"Had willed him emerge and survive, and that slowly,
    through age upon age,

From the jungle and swamp to the city the painful
    ascent should be made,
From the first rude stammer of tongues to the speech
    of the poet and sage,
From the first rough knottings of barter to infinite
    network of trade;

" From isolate weakness to fagoted strength in the
    communal band,
To the peace and justice of States from the clashings
    of wilderness-wars;
From the fingers that fashioned the flint to the fingers
    of Raphael's hand;
From the skulls that bleach in the caves to the
    heads that have measured the stars;

" To the end that at last—that at last the whole into
    night should go down
Into night and the void, when the long-sought sum-
    mit of things has been won,

And the glorious God-planned scheme attain consum-
    mation and crown
In the idiot whirl of a lifeless globe round a useless
    sun ? "

Yet once more the Voice whose tones
Froze the marrow in my bones :—
" Can it be, O can it be,
(Cry the ants in agony,)
That the power whose prescient mind
Our illustrious race designed,
Placed us here with cunning blest
To construct our mighty nest,
And to store our yearly fruit,
Also foreordained the Boot
That with catastrophic——"
                " Nay,
Spare your sneers.   Far happier they,
In that only fancy sees
Power in them for thoughts like these :

In that whatsover fate
Their frail race annihilate
To despair it will condemn
No immortal hopes in them.
But for *us !*   O God of truth,
God of justice and of ruth !
Does our everlasting wrong
To thy equity belong ?
Did thy truth decree on high
That we should believe a lie ?
And is thy compassion shown
In a truth too late made known ?
Why to man alone this lot ?"
Cried the Voice : "And know'st thou not ?"
Then, in words of bitter gibe—
" Claims not man's complacent tribe
O'er the beasts pre-eminence,
Chief in this—his laughter-sense ?
So the fate contrived for him
Should appeal, in humour grim,

To that faculty acute
Which discerns him from the brute :
Wherefore hopes and longings blind
Were enkindled in his mind,
And to fire's devouring strength
Fanned and fostered—that at length
Their evanishment in smoke
Might produce the effect of joke ! "

" Ah, scoffer accursed ! " I cried, " we know and too
    well we know

  How cruel a humour indulges the Power who
    breathed in us breath,

How he bred in us love of our children and wives
    and rooted it so

  That our hearts are transfixed by the point of the
    terrible jest of death !

" We know " (and my voice sank lower) " he even
    refines upon this,

And deludes us with shadowy hopes of meetings
    beyond the grave,
Though as yet he has spared undeceiving the weak
    and prolongs them the bliss
    Of the faith that he slowly tears from the tortured
        breasts of the brave !

"But must we believe at your bidding that 'life-in-
    the-future of earth'
    Is the nothing of life-in-the-heavens? that *that* last
        pitiful gleam
Is to fade from the sky of the soul, till the great World
    Jester his mirth
    Shall have sated on anguish of man in dispersing
        the Humanist dream ?"

    No answer came.   I cried again ;
      No voice the silence broke
    Till silence seemed to burst my brain,
      And, sweating cold, I woke.

I woke : long hours had fled, and lo !
   Dim-seen through curtains drawn,
The moon's pale corpse is sinking slow
   In the grey pools of dawn.
Night is departing terror-thronged,
   But unreleased I seem,
For waking life awhile prolonged
   The questionings of dream,
And break of day the hour had brought
   That bows the soul to earth
In idle travail of a thought
   Which comes not to the birth ;
So to the voice that answered not
   Still cried I " Answer Thou !
The dumb enigma of our lot
   Lies heaviest on us now."
But now ! . . . The brooding East was riven,
   The morning-wind took wing,
 Above in the fast-brightening heaven
   The lark began to sing ;

Sweet through the lattice breathed the bine,
    The mower clinked his scythe;
Rang out from 'mid the gathered kine
    The milkmaid's laughter blithe.

Ah! blessèd sounds of wiser life,
    Contented with its day,
How ye rebuke the inward strife
    That wears the soul away!

And blessèd life itself! that holds,
    So we not shun its grasp,
The troubled spirits it enfolds
    In soothing mother-clasp;

Whose commonplaces merciful
    The brain from madness keep,
And lull—so we but let them lull—
    Until we fall asleep.

PRINTED BY WILLIAM BLACKWOOD AND SONS.

SELECTED LIST.

LITTLE COMEDIES : OLD AND NEW. By JULIAN STURGIS, Author of 'John-a-Dreams,' 'An Accomplished Gentleman,' &c. Crown 8vo, 7s. 6d.

" A very clever and charming book."—*Truth.*

" Delicate and charming 'Little Comedies.'"—*Pall Mall Gazette.*

" There is a graceful play of fancy, a delicacy of touch, a refinement of humour, in these 'Little Comedies,' which make them very acceptable to those who are capable of appreciating such attractions."—*John Bull.*

THE WORKS OF HORACE. Translated into English Verse. With a Life and Notes. By SIR THEODORE MARTIN, K.C.B. Two volumes, post 8vo, printed on hand-made paper, 21s.

" No version of Horace has ever appeared in England more complete in itself or more likely to be popular than the one which Sir Theodore Martin has now given to the public."—*Athenæum.*

BON GAULTIER'S BOOK OF BALLADS. By Professor AYTOUN and SIR THEODORE MARTIN. Thirteenth Edition. With Illustrations by DOYLE, LEECH, and CROWQUILL. Post 8vo, gilt edges, 8s. 6d.

THE BALLADS OF SCOTLAND. Edited by Professor AYTOUN. Fourth Edition. 2 vols. fcap. 8vo, 12s.

LAYS OF THE SCOTTISH CAVALIERS, AND OTHER POEMS. By W. EDMONDSTOUNE AYTOUN, D.C.L., Professor of Rhetoric and Belles-Lettres in the University of Edinburgh. Twenty-eighth Edition. Fcap. 8vo, 7s. 6d.

AN ILLUSTRATED EDITION OF THE LAYS OF THE SCOTTISH CAVALIERS. From Designs by Sir NOEL PATON. Small 4to, 21s. in gilt cloth.

SONGS AND VERSES, SOCIAL AND SCIENTIFIC. By AN OLD CONTRIBUTOR TO 'MAGA.' Fifth Edition, fcap. 8vo, 4s.

ORELLANA, AND OTHER POEMS. By J. Logie Rob-
ERTSON, M.A. Fcap. 8vo. Printed on hand-made paper, 6s.

"'Orellana' is an epic based on the Spanish conquests in America, and is full
of fire and vigour.... In the rest of the book there are many clever and amusing
poems."—*Whitehall Review*.

GOETHE'S FAUST. Translated by Sir Theodore Martin,
K.C.B. Second Edition, crown 8vo, 6s. Cheap Edition, 3s. 6d.

POEMS AND BALLADS OF HEINRICH HEINE. By the
Same. Done into English Verse. Second Edition. Printed on
papier vergé, crown 8vo, 8s.

GRAFFITI D'ITALIA. By W. W. Story, Author of 'Roba
di Roma.' Second Edition, fcap. 8vo, 7s. 6d.

NERO; A Historical Play. By the Same. Fcap. 8vo, 6s.

SONGS OF BÉRANGER done into English Verse. By
WILLIAM YOUNG. New Edition, revised. Fcap. 8vo, 4s. 6d.

POEMS AND TRANSCRIPTS. By Eugene Lee-Hamil-
TON. Crown 8vo, 6s.

LAYS AND LEGENDS OF ANCIENT GREECE. By
JOHN STUART BLACKIE, Professor of Greek in the University
of Edinburgh. Second Edition. Fcap. 8vo, 5s.

THE COMEDY OF THE NOCTES AMBROSIANÆ. By
CHRISTOPHER NORTH. Edited by John Skelton, Advocate.
With a Portrait of Professor Wilson and of the Ettrick Shepherd,
engraved on Steel. Crown 8vo, 7s. 6d.

WILLIAM BLACKWOOD & SONS, Edinburgh and London.